Henry Roe

Story of the First Hundred Years of the Diocese of Quebec

Henry Roe

Story of the First Hundred Years of the Diocese of Quebec

ISBN/EAN: 9783337326951

Printed in Europe, USA, Canada, Australia, Japan

Cover: Foto ©Andreas Hilbeck / pixelio.de

More available books at **www.hansebooks.com**

STORY

OF THE

First Hundred Years

OF THE

Diocese of Quebec,

BY THE

Venerable HENRY ROE, D.D.,

Archdeacon of Quebec.

———◆•◆◀▶◆•◆———

QUEBEC:

PRINTED AT THE "MORNING CHRONICLE" OFFICE.

1893.

PREFACE.

The sources of the following narrative, besides the writer's personal reminiscences extending over fifty years, are the following :

Sketch of the life of the first Bishop of Quebec, by his son the third Bishop, in the Christian Remembrancer for the year 1825, Vol. vii, p. 591 ff.

Memoir of Colonel Armine Mountain by his widow.

Norton's Sketch of the life of Bishop Stewart.

Bishop Henshaw's Reminiscences of Bishop Stewart.

Mrs. Day's History of the Settlement of the Eastern Townships.

Memoir of Bishop G. J. Mountain, by his son the Rev. A. W. Mountain. This Memoir leaves nothing to be desired for the period it covers.

The Rev. Jacob Mountain's work in Newfoundland, with sketch of his life, by Canon Carter, of Clewer.

Annals of the Dioceses of Quebec and Toronto, by the Rev. Ernest Hawkins.

Pascoe's Digest of the S. P. G. Records from 1701 to 1892.

Brymner's Papers from the Dominion Archives on the Early History of Canada, 2 Vols.

Life of General Simcoe.

LENNOXVILLE,
      Whitsun Monday, 1893.

STORY

FIRST HUNDRED YEARS OF THE DIOCESE OF QUEBEC.

CHAPTER I.

THE FIRST BISHOP OF QUEBEC:

DR. JACOB MOUNTAIN, A.D., 1793-1825.

The work of laying the foundations of the Canadian Church was committed in the Providence of God to a Prelate worthy of the trust. The selection of the man for this high responsibility fell to the great English statesman, the younger Pitt; and he chose Dr. Jacob Mountain, then vicar of Brockden and Prebendary, of Lincoln, being guided in his choice by the celebrated Dr. Tomline, Bishop of Lincoln, whose examining chaplain and friend Dr. Mountain was.

Of the thirty-two years of devoted service of their first Bishop, mainly owing to his own modest reticence and self repression, Canadian churchmen know but little. Sufficient, however, can be traced out to make it certain that a large proportion of whatever has been, in the truest sense of the word, *success* in the life of the Canadian Church, may be fairly traced to him.

Dr. Mountain was consecrated in Lambeth Palace Chapel on the 7th July, 1793, and almost immediately sailed for his new home.

The late Dean Bethune, " who had known all of the name who had sojourned in Canada," said to one of them: " The Mountains are remarkable for two things, charity to the poor and abstinence from wine." The Dean might have added a third characteristic,— an unusual depth and tenderness of family affection. The strength of this last trait was evidenced by the whole Mountain family resolving to accompany the Bishop to Canada and to cast in their lot with him there.

The party was composed of thirteen Mountains,— the Bishop's elder brother Jehoshaphat and his son Salter, both of them in holy orders ; the Bishop and his three sons, then almost infants ; the rest of the family were of the gentler sex. After a voyage of thirteen weeks of great hardship and peril, they landed at Quebec on All Saints' Day.

It will be readily understood that the position of Dr. Mountain as the first Canadian Bishop, was one involving many difficulties. First, to lay well and soundly the foundations of the church in a new world,—to adapt the traditions of the great State Church of England to an infant country,—to know when to modify her rules and when to stand firm, called for much wise judgment. He had also other duties which exposed him to the danger of public odium ; he was *ex-officio* a member of the Executive and Legislative Councils, and was frequently called to sit as a judge in the Court of Appeals. These duties he discharged with such integrity and singleness of purpose as to win universal confidence, while his services to the state on some important occasions were publicly acknowledged by the several Governors.

The discouragements which he had to face in his spiritual work were very great. He found himself, on the one hand, in the capital city of a Province, settled and cultivated now for a century and a quarter by an industrious, thriving, contented and religious people; confronted with a church thoroughly organized and a clergy loved and respected, and supported handsomely by their own parishioners. When he looked on the other hand at the material out of which he was required to build up the Church of England in Canada, the comparison was, and was felt to be, depressing:—the whole British race in both Provinces, some 15,000 in number, and so widely scattered as to require for their visitation a circuit of some 3,000 miles;—the large majority of them, dissenters from the Church of England; and even of her own attached sons, not one probably having the faintest idea that it was his duty to make any personal sacrifice for her support; no Ecclesiastical building of any kind in his whole diocese, excepting one church;—with nine clergy only, and not every one of them respected or respectable.

The morals of the new Bishop's flock did not stand high. The Venerable Roman Catholic Bishop Briand welcomed Bishop Mountain with a kiss on both cheeks, but remarked significantly: "Your presence was much needed to keep your people in order." And twenty-five years earlier,—but it is to be hoped things had improved since then,—Governor Murray, in a despatch to the Home Government, says of the Protestants of Montreal and Quebec,—excepting only a few half-pay officers,—" I report them to be in general the most immoral collection of men I ever knew,"

The Bishop's coming was well timed to the moral and spiritual wants of the country. The foundations of Canadian Society, under the new regime, were only being laid. In Lower Canada, the English were as yet few in numbers and were found mainly in the towns of Quebec, Three Rivers, Sorel and Montreal; apart from these, scarcely an attempt at settlement had as yet been made. The Bishop found nine clergymen in the country, six in Lower and three in Upper Canada. The six clergy were all in the towns of the Lower Province, and were probably not inadequate in number to its wants.

In Upper Canada it was different. The country parts were beginning to fill in rapidly. At the close of his first visitation in 1794, the Bishop writes that " from the point which separates the two Provinces and upwards, the progress of population and cultivation was astonishing "; and he adds that " the mass of the settlers were entirely destitute of the means of religious instruction and observed no forms of public worship." In the whole two hundred miles between Montreal and Kingston, all of which was comparatively well settled, there was not a single church or a single clergyman. A chaplain at Niagara, then the seat of Government, a clergyman at Kingston, and one travelling missionary formed the entire clergy of the Upper Province.

SUPPLY OF THE NEEDED CLERGY.

The Bishop at once set himself with energy to supply the more pressing of these wants. His own brother placed first at Three Rivers, and subsequently at Montreal, and his nephew, the much-loved Salter Mountain, Bishop's Chaplain, and for twenty-years Rector of Quebec, were an invaluable addition to the staff.

The difficulty of providing funds to pay the additional clergy needed was great, but far greater the difficulty of finding suitable men. No one thought of calling upon the people to support their own church. It was taken for granted that in an Established Church the clergy should be paid by the Government. Indeed such provision was supposed to have been made when the Clergy Reserves were set apart ; but they never became available to any extent in Lower Canada. They were a source of weakness rather than of strength to the church. Besides the odium their possession brought upon her, an immense amount of time and energy was wasted in contending for them, which might have been much better employed.

With the generous help, however, of the S. P. G., the Bishop was enabled gradually to increase the number of the clergy and to keep the extension of the Church in some degree in pace with the advancing settlement of the country. At his decease, in 1825, he left sixty-one clergymen (including three Archdeacons) where he had found nine, forty-eight of them being missionaries of the S. P. G.

Educating Clergy in the Country.

Some of the best of these missionaries were men found and ordained in the country, who thus began their ministry with experience of Canadian life, which was invaluable. The Bishop soon saw the necessity of looking to the country itself to supply him with Clergy, and began to take measures for their regular training. The Society here again came to his aid, and, in 1815, placed the sum of £200 stg. a year at his disposal for the support of four students in Divinity while pursuing their studies with clergymen of ability and experience.

This system, the precursor of the more developed Divinity Schools of to-day, the Bishop left in working order at his death. Dr. A. N. Bethune, afterwards Bishop of Toronto, in Upper Canada, and the Rev. Joseph Braithwaite, of Chambly, and the Rev. Samuel Simpson Wood, of Three Rivers, in Lower Canada, did much good service in this responsible work. Among those so ordained, by the first Bishop of Quebec, with more or less of previous training, were Dr. John Strachan, the first, and Dr. Alexander Neil Bethune, the second Bishop of Toronto ; Dr. John Bethune, elder brother of the latter, the first Dean of Montreal ; Dr. James Reid, the successor of Bishop Stewart at Frelighsburg, and his son, Dr. Charles Peter Reid, Rector of Sherbrooke ; George Archbold, the saintly successor of Bishop Stewart in his work as visiting missionary ; and most distinguished of them all, his own son George, afterwards the third Bishop of Quebec.

BUILDING OF CHURCH EDIFICES.

There was the same destitution as to churches, parsonages and schools. In Quebec, Montreal, Kingston or Toronto, there was not a single ecclesiastical building of any kind. There was a church at Sorel and the foundation laid of another at Niagara. The clergy officiated in court-houses or in churches " borrowed " from the Church of Rome. This want, too, the Bishop set himself to remedy with the like success, and at his death left in his diocese nearly 60 churches " built or in progress or fairly undertaken." Towards four of the most important of these, the Bishop obtained a grant of £1,000 stg. from the Home Government. And towards them all liberal grants were made by the Society, besides his own generous contributions.

The entire credit, however, for the building of his own Cathedral must be conceded to himself. The money came from the British chest, but it was drawn out by the urgent representations of the Bishop, backed up by the influence of his warm personal friend the Governor. The Cathedral of Quebec still remains one of the most satisfactory churches for worship in Canada ; its acoustic properties are perfect. The grant in the name of the King was for "a *Metropolitan* Church," indicating the intention of the Government to make Quebec the Metropolitan See. The Bishop's hope was to establish at once a regular Cathedral Establishment, and he urged strongly upon the Government the propriety and wisdom of making provision by endowment for a Dean and Chapter. He failed in this part of his project ; but, nevertheless, he provided at once upon its opening a surpliced Choir and a choral service, the expenses being defrayed out of the pew rents. Some twenty years after his death, the surpliced Choir was allowed to fall through.

TRIENNIAL VISITATIONS.

The regular triennial Visitation of the diocese was of course the most important of the Bishop's functions. These entailed much hardship. The roads in many parts were only beginning to be opened up, and so far as they did exist, were incredibly bad. There were no regular public conveyances. In Upper Canada, travelling was mostly by water in schooners, barges and canoes. And this involved also great expense. There is incidental mention of the cost of one canoe voyage of the Bishop from Montreal to Detroit ; exclusive of provisions it amounted to $600. The Bishop felt it his duty to keep up, so far as possible, on these circuits, something of the state maintained by the Bishops in England, " holding that his salary was given him, not for his private benefit, but as the means of usefulness and also to maintain the dignity of the Episcopal office." To his honour, be it said, that he did spend the whole of his income upon his work, leaving at his death nothing to his wife and daughters, save his own slender private fortune.

Eight times the Bishop went over his Diocese,—each circuit involving more than 8,000 miles of travel,—penetrating on each occasion to every spot where a mission had been opened, confirming the young, stimulating the zeal of the clergy, promoting the building of churches and the extension of the church in every way, and, above all, seeking to deepen the religious life of the people. His confirmation addresses and sermons, as well as his charges to the clergy, coming as they did from the greatest preacher of the age, and illustrated as they were by his own beautiful life, could not fail to leave permanent impressions. Not only were his confirmation addresses extempore—his sermons also on these circuits frequently were so. " If I could do it as well," remarks his son George on one occasion, " I should never address a country congregation in any other way."

THE BISHOP'S EFFORTS ON BEHALF OF EDUCATION.

Bishop Mountain's earnest and persistent efforts on behalf of EDUCATION ought not to be passed over in silence. He advocated a general scheme of a University and Grammar Schools for the whole country, endowed and fostered by the Government, and in organic connexion with the " Established Protestant Episcopal Church of the Country," He never ceased to press this project upon the attention of the several Governors, though he failed to secure its adoption. *

The foundation of McGill College is directly due to him. He secured for it a Royal Charter, and on his arrival submitted a plan for its establishment as a University to the Governor in Chief, Lord Dalhousie, by whom it was approved. The will, however, having been contested, the establishment of the College was delayed.

Planting of the Church in the Eastern Townships.

In the earlier years of his Episcopate, the Bishop's visitations in Lower Canada were confined to the towns and the few settlements in the *Seigneuries*. The English-speaking settlement of the Province had scarcely begun. The Eastern Townships were the only part of the country of much value left unoccupied by the French, and at that time they were an unbroken wilderness. At the beginning of the century, emigrants began to pour rapidly into these Townships, mostly from the neighbouring States. A fair proportion of the settlers were U. E. Loyalists ; the greater number were simply attracted by the Government's liberal offers of free grants of land. But, however politically affected, they were nearly all imbued with strong Puritanical views and prejudices.

Charles James Stewart, the Apostle of the Townships.

The first effort on the part of the Church to provide for the religious wants of these people, was by send-

---

* See Bishop George Mountain's Memoir of Bishop Jacob Mountain in the Christian Remembrancer, Vol. vii, page 592. Correspondence of the first Bishop of Quebec with Governor Simcoe. Also, Memoir of Bishop George Mountain by his son, pp. 64-66.

ing the Rev. R. Q. Short in 1800, and in 1804, the Rev. C. C. Cotton, as missionaries of the S. P. G., to Missisquoi Bay. The true Apostle of the Townships, however, was CHARLES JAMES STEWART, afterwards the second Bishop of Quebec.

The Hon. and Rev. Charles James Stewart, fifth son of the Earl of Galloway, a fellow of All Souls, and also, besides his independent fortune, holding a wealthy benefice in England, felt inwardly moved to devote himself to missionary work. While considering the claims of India, he was attracted, it is said, by a printed appeal put forth by Bishop Mountain, then in England, portraying the spiritual destitution of his Diocese. Mr. Stewart at once called on the Bishop and offered his services. He came to Canada in the autumn of 1807, and was sent to relieve Mr. Cotton of a portion of his large mission, and settled down at Frelighsburg. From this point as a centre he laboured for eight years in the Townships west of Lake Memphremagog, now part of the Diocese of Montreal, with wonderful success in gathering the people into the church and reforming their lives. Then, satisfied that the pastoral care of those he had won could be entrusted to other hands, he first made two extensive circuits of exploration on the east side of the Lake, searching out the religious condition and needs of the people in what is now the Counties of Stanstead and Compton, and finally selected Hatley as the centre of his labours for that region. The two fields of labour were much the same in extent, there being then, according to Dr. Stewart's computation, a population of more than 7,000 on the west side of the Lake, and about 8,000 on the east side.

Here he was visited in 1819 by Archdeacon Mountain. "I found him," he says, "in occupation of a small garret in a wooden house reached by a sort of ladder. Here he had one room in which were his little open bed, his books and his writing table. And here, buried in the wood, this simple and single-hearted man, very far from strong in bodily health, was labouring to build up the Church of God among a population utter strangers to the Church of England with the exception of a single family."

The same remarkable success crowned his labours here. His stay at Hatley was only for two years, and yet in that time he had won the confidence and affection of all classes, and seemed to have leavened the whole country from Stanstead to Compton with the Church's doctrine and discipline.

But he was not content to rest there. He felt that he had gifts for pioneer work which might be utilized in a larger field. " My experience," he says, in a letter to his sister, " suits me for the business. My being single is a great advantage to me as a missionary on a large scale. I am always ready to go or stay anywhere for a long or a short time ; and no place and every place is my home. My personal expenses are so small. I reckon that those of myself and my servant come now to about £250 a year—this leaves me of my income £400 a year for public and private benevolent purposes." Accordingly, in 1820, he again passed on his work to another, and for himself solicited and obtained from the society an office he had persuaded them to create, which he called his ' promotion,'—the post of Visiting Missionary for the whole of Upper and Lower Canada. In this truly apostolic work he laboured, with never flagging enthusiasm, and immense advantage to the church, down to Bishop Mountain's death, searching out, in all the new settlements of both Provinces, the most promising fields for establishing missions of the church, and, where there were no funds from other sources, securing by his influence in England the money necessary to pay the additional missionaries and to build the churches that were needed.

It was the great merit as well as happiness of the first Bishop of Quebec, to have had men so deeply and yet so soundly and soberly religious for his lieutenants almost throughout his entire episcopate,—Dr. Stewart from the year 1807, his son George since 1811.

Archdeacon Mountain's Pioneer Work.

The work so well begun by Dr. Stewart, of leavening the Eastern Townships while they were in process of settlement with sound religious influences, was taken up and carried on with equal zeal by his younger contemporary and friend, Dr. George Mountain. For the last seven years of his father's life, he was Official of the Diocese; for the last four, Archdeacon.

During these years the Archdeacon made circuits through the Townships again and again, visiting all the settlements where there were openings for the church, collecting the people together and instructing them in the church's ways in those wonderful extemporaneous addresses which did so much to dissipate their prejudices and win them to her fold.

The Religious Influence of the Mountain Family.

And here, perhaps, is the right place to say, what ought to be said, that the benefit of highest value which Bishop Jacob Mountain conferred upon the Canadian Church was the *religious* influence which he brought to it in his own person and in his family.

The Mountain family have been to this church and country, in the silent secret influence of their personal religion, "the very salt of the earth." It is not too

much to say, speaking of those who have finished their
course, that every member of the Mountain family,
both male and female, has borne in some real degree
the stamp of *saintliness*.

The limited space of this memoir will not permit
the grounds of this assertion to be fully traced out, but
one proof may be offered. In the higher classes of
society, in cases where other honourable and lucrative
callings are open to a man's sons, there is no surer sign
of a true inward value for religion than his giving those
sons, and their giving themselves, to the sacred ministry.
Bishop Jacob Mountain and his elder and only brother Jehoshaphat were clergymen. Of the elder of these
brothers, all the male descendants, the only son in
each of three generations, have been clergymen. Three
of Bishop Jacob Mountain's four sons devoted themselves to the same sacred office. One of the three had
no children. Of the other two, the only son of Dr. Jacob
Mountain, and the eldest son of Dr. George Mountain,
followed the same example. And all of these who have
passed away were saintly men, some of them preem-
inently so. Salter Mountain's life in Cornwall; Bishop
George Mountain's life in Quebec; his son Armine
Mountain's twenty years in Canada; his cousin Jacob
Mountain's life in Newfoundland, were shining examples of the highest walking with God; while the
only two Mountains who embraced secular callings,
both gallant soldiers, were equally attractive and beautiful examples of the very best type of personal religion.

It will readily be felt how deeply the secret leaven of
such good examples, exerted unbrokenly for three quarters of a century, must have influenced the life of the
church in Canada, and with what valuable results. If
there is in the religious life of the Diocese of Quebec

2

to-day anything on which the hearts of its members
can rest with comfort and thankfulness, anything
that is lovely, anything of good report, they know
at least one source to which to trace it.

THE CHARACTER OF THE FIRST BISHOP OF QUEBEC.

The character of the first Bishop of Quebec has been
drawn by two of his children, Bishop George Mountain
and Colonel Armine Mountain, both in the best
position to compare him with the leading men of the
age. After making all necessary deduction for affectionate partiality, there can be no doubt that he was
a man of a singularly noble and beautiful character,
most affectionately lovable, profoundly religious, of the
most transparent integrity and uprightness.

" Our father lives in my recollection," writes Colonel
Mountain, " as a being of a higher order and a different
race from the men " (the noblest and best of the age)
" among whom my life has been passed. He was not only
essentially a gentleman, but I have never, in all my
wanderings, seen a prince who had his bearing. He
united to all the true dignity of a Bishop, a kindness and
tenderness peculiar to himself and the easy grace of a
highly accomplished man,—at once manly and mild,
and full of sparkling conversation. In the pulpit I have
never heard his equal ; his fine countenance and noble
figure, his sonorous and melodious voice, his impressive
action, produced an effect which none who ever heard
him can forget. There was no escaping from that voice ;
it searched into every corner of the church, and every
other sound was hushed......He was in truth, the most
princely-minded, the most highly-gifted, the kindest,
noblest, most strictly upright, simple-hearted human
being I have ever known."

And his son George writes of him : * " Never was a character more perfectly *genuine*, more absolutely elevated above all artifice or pretension, more thoroughly averse from all ostentation in religion. In his public performance of the functions proper to the Episcopal office, the commanding dignity of his person, the impressive seriousness of his manner, the felicitous propriety of his utterance gave the utmost effect to the beautiful services of the church. In the pulpit, it is not too much to say that the advantage of his fine and venerable aspect, the grace, force and solemn fervour of his delivery, the power and happy regulation of his tones, the chaste expressiveness of his action, combined with the strength and clearness of his reasoning, the unstudied magnificence of his language, and that piety, that exalted faith in his REDEEMER, which was and shewed itself to be pregnant with the importance of its subject and intent upon conveying the same feeling to others, made him altogether a preacher who has never in modern times been surpassed."

CHURCH PROGRESS IN THE DIOCESE OF QUEBEC.

At the close of the thirty-two years of Bishop Jacob Mountain's Episcopate, marked progress had indeed been made, as we have seen, in supplying the spiritual needs of his vast Diocese ; but, in that portion of it which now forms the Diocese of Quebec, it was still the day of small things.

In the city of Quebec there were four clergy, and seven outside of it. The four in the city were the Rector, an assistant, who gave his Sundays to the parts adjacent ; a military chaplain ; and the incumbent of

* The Christian Remembrancer, Vol. vii, page 594.

a proprietary chapel. The seven outside the city were the Rectors of Three Rivers and Drummondville; three missionaries in the District of St. Francis, at Hatley, Eaton, and Lennoxville; and two in the District of Gaspé. Of these eleven clergymen, four were paid by the Government, and seven were missionaries of the S. P. G.

Bishop Jacob Mountain, after a very brief illness, was called to his rest on the 18th June, 1825.

CHAPTER II.

THE SECOND BISHOP OF QUEBEC :

BISHOP STEWART, A.D., 1826-1836.

Bishop Jacob Mountain's decease was very unexpected. His health had been much broken for some time, and his son, the Archdeacon, was then in England negotiating with the authorities to afford the Bishop some relief. The Government made great difficulty in acceding to anything which involved the necessity for an additional vote of money, knowing the opposition this would meet with in Parliament. The Bishop desired to retire, but to this the Colonial Minister saw strong objections. Finally, the project of a division of the Diocese was acceded to, Dr. Stewart to be appointed Bishop of Upper Canada, and to give the Bishop of Quebec such assistance as he might need, or, if necessary, to take full charge of the church in both Provinces.

On the death of Bishop Mountain, Dr. Stewart proceeded to England, as had been arranged, for consecration as Bishop of Upper Canada, carrying with him the suffrages of the whole Canadian Church that the Archdeacon should succeed his father as Bishop of Quebec. The Government, however, refused to carry the division of the Diocese into effect, on the ground that it had been rendered necessary only by the failing health of the late Bishop. With all the pressure he could bring to bear, Dr. Stewart failed to alter this decision, the difficulty being, as explained above, that of providing the necessary stipend. Dr. Stewart was therefore consecrated Bishop of Quebec with the charge of the whole of Canada.

The consecration took place on the Feast of the Circumcision, 1826, and in the summer, the new Bishop returned to Canada and at once entered with zeal and energy upon the visitation of his vast Diocese, with every portion of which and its wants he was throughly acquainted.

During the first six years of his Episcopate, the Bishop went over the country, much of it on horseback, from one end to the other very carefully, portions of it two or three times, ordaining, confirming, baptizing, searching out and ministering to its scattered people, much as he had done while a simple missionary.

The Rev. George Archbold.

He did not, however, permit the office of visiting missionary, on which he set so high a value, to fall through. A fitting successor was found in the Rev. George Archbold. Mr. Archbold, cut off alas! in the prime of his usefulness, was another of the noble band of saintly planters of the church to whom Canada owes so much. Archdeacon Mountain's characterization of him in a private letter written about this time may well be put on record here ; he speaks of Mr. Archbold as "this unaffectedly devoted servant of God and His Church, who is an example to us all ; so zealous, so devout, so humble, so genuine, so single-hearted, so entirely given to the work to which he is called, it does one good to be in contact with him, and we may well desire to learn from him."

PROGRESS OF THE CHURCH IN UPPER CANADA.

The harvest in Canada was plenteous in those days, but the labourers were few indeed. The Upper Province particularly was yearly receiving large accessions to its population. During these ten years, some 300,000 English emigrants came to the N. A. Colonies, most of them to Canada. The population of Upper Canada, in 1826, was 164,000; in 1835, it had more than doubled, having increased to 337,000. It was the church's opportunity. About one third of the people claimed to belong to her fold, and multitudes of others were ready to be gathered in. But, with all the exertions of the true-hearted men who were in command, the clergy in the Upper Province, at Bishop Stewart's retirement, had only increased to fifty-one. There was a lack of money, but a still more serious lack of men.

THE STEWART MISSION FUND.

For money, Dr. Stewart had made strenuous efforts to add to the help received from the S. P. G. There was first a more private fund formed for helping him, while Visiting Missionary, in providing clergy for the more destitute places and in building churches. This was called the Stewart Mission Fund, and was in the hands of a personal friend in England, the Rev. W. J. D. Waddilove. It was the means of maintaining travelling missionaries in Upper Canada for many years, and also afforded some help in Lower Canada.

THE UPPER CANADA CLERGY SOCIETY.

Towards the close of his Episcopate, Bishop Stewart took steps for establishing a society on a larger scale, to help in the work of Canadian Missions. It was called the Upper Canada Clergy Society, its chief supporter in England being his nephew, the Earl of Galloway. The completion of its organization, however, devolved upon Bishop Stewart's successor, who, while in England for his consecration, secured for it the adhesion of the Bishop of London, and successfully launched it. This society did good service for a time. Some years later it was, by Bishop Mountain's advice, merged in the S. P. G.

Beginnings of Canadian self-help.

The duty of helping themselves out of their own resources, however, was not quite forgotten by Canadian churchmen. Somewhat earlier, a society had been organized in Quebec and Toronto, called The Upper Canada Travelling Missionary Fund for the Propagation of the Gospel among destitute settlers and Indians, a branch of which was afterwards established at Montreal. Each branch maintained a travelling Missionary. This was the first attempt at organization for self-help on the part of the Canadian Church.

Dr. Stewart continued his labours with the same ardent zeal until his health began to fail. Indeed the oversight of so vast a field was quite too much for any man.

The Labours of Archdeacon Mountain.

He had, however, a strong man at his right hand. Archdeacon Mountain was, all through Bishop Stewart's administration, a most important factor in the growth and development of the church. No one knew this better than the Bishop himself, who "leaned upon his friend for advice and assistance in all that he undertook," and made free use of his pen in most if not

all of the Pastoral Addresses which he sent forth.
Indeed the whole Diocese was permeated with the
influence of the burning zeal, and meek piety, and splen-
didly successful work of the Archdeacon. His chief
field of labour was of course his own parish of Quebec,
which included the whole city, with a church population of 5,000 souls, and which he made by his amazing
pastoral activity and holy example, a model parish,
such as few parishes have ever been.

THE CHOLERA OF 1832.

In the centre of the last ten years of his Rectorship
came the fearful invasion of Cholera in 1832. His heroic devotion in meeting the plague won for him the
highest place in the admiration and gratitude of the
entire community. The pestilence took a most aggravated form, and the sufferings and terror of the people
were awful beyond description. In little more than two
months, one tenth of the population of Quebec, which
then numbered 28,000, was carried off. The number of
interments by the Rector and his one assistant in that
year was 975, the Rector himself burying more than
seventy bodies in two consecutive days. He never left
his post for a day, and the whole of his time was given
up to ministering to the sick and dying. And not in
the city only, the country round Quebec for miles had
no other clergyman to look to for spiritual consolation.
" A horse was kept saddled in his stable night and day
to enable him and his curate to meet the calls from a
distance. Their rule was to take night calls alternate-
ly, but on many nights they were both out, and for
whole days together unable to return home." No
wonder that henceforth the love and reverence of the
people for their Rector was beyond expression.

ARCHDEACON MOUNTAIN'S PIONEER WORK IN THE COUNTRY PARTS OF LOWER CANADA.

His work in the city of Quebec, however, even in those years, was far from all. The planting of the church throughout the whole of Lower Canada was largely the result of his personal exertions. He was appointed Archdeacon in 1821, and in 1822 he began his periodical circuits, going over, in that year, the whole of the English settlements in Lower Canada, excepting Gaspé,—visiting, investigating, preaching, baptizing, wherever an opening offered, and reporting to the Bishop and the S. P. G. the spiritual needs of the settlers in his admirable Journals, so charmingly written, several of which were printed in full by the Society.

In 1824 and again in 1826, he visited the District of Gaspé,—the difficulties and hardships involved, as the means of travelling then were, being to us almost inconceivable.

In the years between 1828 and 1832 he again went twice over all the English-speaking settlements of the Province, including in these circuits the more newly-settled townships which now form the District of Megantic.

This record of dates and circuits is sufficiently dry; but its meaning is, that this great Evangelist, for such he was, during the fourteen years that he was Archdeacon, travelled again and again over the whole of Lower Canada, preaching the Gospel of the Grace of God to the crowds who everywhere hung upon his lips, and setting the Church of their fathers, against which and her ways they were most of them deeply prejudiced, before the eyes of the people, in the most beautiful and attractive light. Wherever he went, his instructive and persuasive preaching left permanent impressions. And, in addition to this, he carried his message home, wherever he stayed, even for a meal, by direct personal appeal in private or some good word dropped in season to every one he met. And this personal influence for good, inexpressibly valuable, continued to characterize his visitations over the same ground as Bishop to the end of his life. Very beautiful and touching is the mention in passing of his gathering the three or four sailors and passengers together, morning and evening, on his tedious voyages by schooner to Gaspé for prayers and instruction, and his own self-reproaches that he had not done it better.

A Coadjutor to Bishop Stewart appointed.

The zealous labours of Bishop Stewart were seriously interrupted during the last two or three years of his Episcopate by the breaking down of his bodily powers. The pastoral care of so vast a Diocese was too much for the strongest man. This he felt from the first, and had urged again and again upon the authorities in England the necessity for relief in his Episcopal duties. Failing to effect anything by writing, he prevailed upon Archdeacon Mountain to proceed to England in 1835, and urge the measure upon the Government in person. His desire was that Upper Canada should be set off as a separate See ; but, if this could not be obtained, he asked for a Coadjutor, towards whose stipend he offered to relinquish £1,000 stg. of his own salary.

The personal exertions of the Archdeacon were so far successful that the Government consented to the appointment of a Coadjutor, his stipend to come out of the salary of the Bishop whom he was to relieve. Bishop Stewart, on his own part and that of the whole

Canadian Church, nominated the Archdeacon for the appointment, and the Colonial Minister, Lord Glenelg, offered it to him in the most flattering terms. So deeply however did he feel his unworthiness that he declined it, and it was only after several months of intreaty from the Bishop and persuasion from all quarters that he finally consented. He accepted the office without a permanent salary, (when he first declined, it was thought a permanent stipend could be secured) the £1,000 a year from Bishop Stewart of course ceasing at his death. The consecration took place at Lambeth Palace Chapel, on the 14th February, 1836, at the same time with that of Bishop Broughton, the first Bishop of Australia.

DEATH OF BISHOP STEWART.

In the autumn of 1836, shortly after the arrival in Canada of his Coadjutor, Bishop Stewart returned to England in the hope of recruiting his health. But the faithful soldier of Christ was worn out. "His cheeks (says his old friend Bishop Henshaw, who met him at New-York on his way) were sunken, his limbs shrunken, and his whole frame emaciated. He was suffering from the effects of a partial paralysis." He lingered on into the next year and died on the 13th July, 1837. His end was like his life, full of humility and patience, and child-like faith, and all the sustaining hopes of a true Christian.

Nothing could be more touching than the account given by a distinguished clergyman of a visit to him on one of those last days. " He asked me to read to him the Order for the Visitation of the sick. At the conclusion, he said : ' There is a prayer for a sick child which I have often read ; pray read it now in my behalf. You will of course make the necessary alterations in some of the words as you pass on, but read it all, and weak and aged as I am, I desire to draw near with the guileless spirit of a child unto my God and Saviour.' "

BISHOP STEWART'S CHARACTER.

The portrait of his pure and elevated character has been drawn by many hands, from which the following is a mosaic: His natural gifts were few, his mind neither brilliant nor profound ; he had neither store of learning nor gift of eloquence. His personal appearance was not prepossessing ; his address was abrupt, and his utterance thick and disagreable. What then was it that made his life so useful and his memory so blessed ? It was that none could hold even a brief interview with him and not be satisfied that he was a man of single eye and devoted heart, whose great aim in life was to promote the happiness of man and the glory of God. He was clothed with humility as with a garment. His guilelessness and single-hearted devotion to the work of Christ won love and reverence for him everywhere. His preaching was commonplace, but there was so much *heart* in it that it was extensively useful. " We have had a most wonderful young man here," writes Miss Mountain, on his first arrival in Canada, "who has charmed us all, and indeed even those who were prejudiced against him, I mean Mr. Stewart, who you doubtless know has come to act here as a Missionary, and so unusual an undertaking in a man of family and independence could not by the world in general be attributed to any but an enthusiast and a Methodist. The papers mentioned his coming to convert the Indians. You see the effect of such conduct as his. With no advantages of person or address,

with real disadvantages of voice and manner in the
pulpit, before he left Quebec he gained general respect, and certainly *did* make converts of those who
were disposed at first to call the real goodness of his
design in question. He met with every discouragement
here, except from a very few persons, yet he continued
stedfast in his perseverance."

Charity and kindness to the poor was a conspicuous
feature in Bishop Stewart's character. He spent as
little as possible upon himself and gave away all the
rest of his income. He died possessed of no property,
the whole of his private fortune having been spent in
works of piety and charity.

He was thoroughly happy in his work. "I never
was so much engaged in the exercises of religion
as I have been since I came to St. Armand, and I
never was happier." He also loved his lowly flock
with a warm and tender affection, and found in
their return of that affection the fulfilment of the
Lord's promise : " So does He bless me, that His
Gospel (Mark 10, 29, 30) is in a manner realized to
me ; and I could sometimes almost say with Jesus that
every faithful Christian is my brother and sister and
mother." He never married, having deliberately chosen
the unmarried state, though feeling it to be a sacrifice,
that he might be more free to serve the Lord Christ.
He spent every Friday in retirement, fasting and
prayer, as the Church appointed, and did not hide his
doing so. Men saw the simple reality of his self-denial
and of his religion, and many were won by it to a
better life. " His decease deprived the Church in
Canada," as his successor beautifully expressed it, "of
one who was her boast and her blessing, and the
clergy of a father and a friend."

The increase in the number of clergy in the whole

of Canada, during the ten years of Bishop Stewart's administration was twenty-four, there being now fifty-one in Upper Canada, and thirty-four in Lower Canada. Of these latter, fifteen were in the present Diocese of Quebec, two only having been added to the permanent Missionary staff, one stationed at Leeds and one at Melbourne, both paid by S. P. G. The churches in Lower Canada had increased from twenty to forty-two and were equally divided between the present two Dioceses of that Province. It was still with us the day of small things.

CHAPTER III.

THE THIRD BISHOP OF QUEBEC:

GEORGE JEHOSHAPHAT MOUNTAIN, A.D., 1836-1863.

Dr. George Mountain was appointed to assist the Bishop of Quebec as Coadjutor, under the title of Bishop of Montreal, with the right of succession to the See of Quebec. As, however, Bishop Stewart returned immediately to England, and died a few months later, the charge of the whole Diocese, which still included the two Canadas, devolved upon Bishop Mountain from the first. His work, like that of Bishop Stewart, was on familiar ground, and he set himself to cultivate the vineyard entrusted to him, pouring out upon it without stint the whole wealth of his splendid intellect, always under the guidance and control of the meek wisdom of his devout and loving heart.

His Episcopate extended over twenty-seven years, and under his able administration the church in the Diocese of Quebec grew from infancy to manhood. Indeed, the development of the organization of the entire Canadian Church falls within this period, and the soundness of its principles and healthiness of its tone was largely due to him.

He found himself from the beginning Bishop of all Canada, but he held the charge of the Upper Province for three years only. He made, however, one exhaustive visitation of that Province in 1838, extending over three months of incessant labour and involving

2,500 miles of travel. In it he confirmed 2,000 persons, ordained at three points, and held a Visitation at Toronto, where fifty of the clergy were present at the delivery of his Charge.

State of the Church in Upper Canada in 1838.

At the close of the visitation, the Bishop made a full report upon the state of the church to Lord Durham, the Governor General, who had requested the Bishop to obtain this information for him. From this report we learn that there were then in Upper Canada, 150,000 adherents of the Church of England, 73 clergy and 90 churches. These people were warmly attached to the church, and very eager to obtain her ministrations. But the spiritual destitution was lamentable. Large tracts of country settled with church-people,— several roads fifty miles in length,—and whole counties were without a single clergyman. The authorities were urged to supply these wants. For the Lower Province, fifteen to twenty more clergy would provide for its present needs; but, in Upper Canada, ample employment would be found for an hundred clergymen beyond the existing Establishment. The Bishop closes his report with an earnest appeal for the erection of a separate See in Upper Canada.

The Bishopric of Toronto created.

The result of these importunate representations, so long continued, was, that the next year Bishop Mountain was relieved of the charge of Upper Canada. Archdeacon Strachan, *Clarum et Venerabile Nomen*, accepted the appointment without a stipend, and was consecrated first Bishop of Toronto on St. Bartholomew's Day, 1839.

3

PROGRESS OF THE CHURCH IN LOWER CANADA AS AN UNDIVIDED SEE.

The erection of a separate See at Montreal took place in 1850, and during the fourteen years that intervened Bishop Mountain completed five circuits of the undivided Diocese. It would be quite vain to attempt in this sketch any full account of the work done. Journals of all the circuits were written by the Bishop; several of them were published by the S. P. G., and large extracts from them all are given in Mr. Armine Mountain's admirable Memoir of his father. The Journals are of a high order of merit, and give the best possible picture of the state of the country and of the progress of the church; and also, incidentally, of the Bishop's own deeply religious character and absorption in his sacred duties.

The most important events in the life of the church during these fourteen years were the founding of the Church Society in 1842, the obtaining the Church Temporalities Act in 1843, the founding of Bishop's College in 1845, and the awful visitation of the Ship Fever in 1847.

THE DIOCESAN CHURCH SOCIETY OF QUEBEC.

The history of the Church Society has been told in the JUBILEE MEMOIR published last year. The story of the splendid work the Society has been the instrument of doing for Quebec, and the unexampled success attained in developing and consolidating the finances of the Diocese by means of its organization, reads almost like a fairy tale. Sufficient credit for this success is perhaps scarcely given to Bishop Mountain in the JUBILEE MEMOIR. The establishment of such an organization had been long in his thoughts. The form first proposed was that of a joint Society for Upper and Lower Canada, and for this he drew up, at Bishop Strachan's request, a Constitution and By-Laws, and also made the draft of an Episcopal Address to proceed from both Bishops, setting the project before the churchmen of Canada. It was finally agreed, however, that there should be a separate Society for each Diocese, though the two were incorporated in one Act of Parliament, and, owing to severe illness from which Bishop Mountain suffered in the winter of 1841-42, the Toronto Society was actually launched in April 1842, that of Quebec not till the 7th July of that year.

Bishop Mountain always looked upon the establishment of the Church Society as a very great benefit to the Church. For the twenty years of his presidency, he gave it his undivided devotion. He himself, and his family were very large contributors to its funds. It was also doubtless due to the noble example of self-sacrifice which his whole life exhibited that the body of laymen whom he attracted around him in its management were men of so high a stamp. He sent the Treasurers of the Society and other members of the Central Board a special message of thanks from his death-bed. To him and to them as working together in the Society in those early days is largely due the strength and independence of the Diocese of Quebec in financial matters to-day.*

BISHOP MOUNTAIN'S VISIT TO RUPERT'S LAND.

In 1844, the Bishop made his memorable visit to Rupert's Land, a voyage by canoe of 3,600 miles, in

---

* "The names of these excellent laymen,—among whom stand prominent Henry S. Scott, Wm. G. Wurtele, James Bell Forsyth, Robert Hamilton, H. N. Jones, R. H. Smith, C. N. Montizambert, George Irvine, W. Darling Campbell, F. H. Anderson,—deserve to be had in everlasting remembrance."—Jubilee Memoir, p. 13.

which he not only carried to that Great Lone Land for the first time the inestimable gifts of Confirmation,—confirming nearly a thousand of the Church's Indian converts,—and Ordination, and in many other respects "the fulness of the blessing of the Gospel of Christ," but also undoubtedly secured, by the unceasing efforts with which he followed it up, the appointment of a Bishop for that Territory in 1849.

THE UNIVERSITY OF BISHOP'S COLLEGE.

The establishment of a College for the training of his clergy had long been in the Bishop's thoughts. He brought the project before the S. P. G. in 1839, and the Society at once voted £200 a year towards the maintenance of Divinity Students in it. The first intention was to place it at Three Rivers under the Rev. S. S. Wood. The final decision was that the true place for such a College was in the midst of the largest English-speaking section of the Province, and so the present site was chosen. On the 18th September, 1845, the corner stone of the College was laid, and in the same month the work of teaching began in a small rented house in Lennoxville, under the charge of JASPER HUME NICOLLS, Michel Fellow of Queen's College, Oxford. Mr. Nicolls was a nephew of the Bishop, but his uncle had no higher stipend to offer the first Principal than £100 a year. Few men have less sought their own than Jasper Nicolls, and perhaps the smallness of the stipend made it more clear to him that it was his duty to accept the offer. He remained at the head of the institution thirty-two years, down to his death, and was succeeded for eight years by DR. JOSEPH LOBLY, of Trinity College, Cambridge. Under their presidency the College grew, not without many trials and vicissitudes, to be the great power for good it now is in the Canadian Church. Dr. Nicolls and Dr. Lobly were both men of singular elevation and purity of character, both great teachers, both greatly beloved, both true sons of the Church of England; and both left the stamp of their own transparent honesty and truth, as well as of their deep personal religion, upon all receptive souls who were so happy as to come under their influence.

In 1853, a Royal charter was granted by the Queen, under which the University of Bishop's College was organized, which now takes its place as one of the four great Universities of old Canada, with its Faculties, so far, of Divinity, Arts and Medicine in full working order, under the able rule of its " honoured lord and Chancellor," DR. HENEKER.

Besides the large number of faithful and able ministers of Christ who have been trained in this noble institution, the College, and the School which has always formed a part of it, have, without question, been eminently successful in imparting to its Alumni the culture of Christian gentlemen, and have been in many ways a power for good in both Church and State in Canada.

THE MARTYR CLERGY OF 1847.

No sketch of the history of the Diocese of Quebec could pass over in silence the heroism with which the Bishop and his clergy jeoparded their lives during the awful visitation of Ship Fever in 1847.

In the spring of that year, following upon the fearful Irish famine of the winter of 1846, tens of thousands of poor famine stricken Irish emigrants fled to Canada bringing with them typhus fever in its most malignant form, were carried ashore out of the emigrant vessels at our Quarantine station of Grosse Isle, and there died in thousands. No language could adequately describe the horrors of the months of that awful summer. The island was almost literally covered with the poor dying people, men, women and children ; the Emigrant Sheds, the Churches, every available building, nearly one hundred tents overflowed with them, and many were lying in the open air. There were for much of the time as many as seventeen or eighteen hundred down with the fever on the Island, and half as many more afloat in the ships for whom room could not be found ashore. The description of the scenes given in extracts from the Bishop's private letters printed in his Memoir, —the suffering, the filth, the sickening stenches, the cries of the dying people, the wailing of orphans,—is most heartrending. The heroic Bishop met this awful irruption of plague, as he had met the inroad of Cholera fifteen years before, with a calm courage, which communicated itself to others. Taking the first turn at Grosse Isle himself, after Mr. Forest, the chaplain for the season, was prostrated by the disease, and a second later on, he invited such of the clergy of the Diocese as seemed most able for the service, to offer themselves for the work of ministering to their poor dying fellow creatures, each to take one week. To this call fourteen of the clergy responded. It was surely a sublime devotion for men to leave their own quiet, healthy country parishes, their wives and their children, and go far away down into the valley of death in that lonely plague-stricken island.

Of the fifteen clergymen of our church, (being the only Protestant ministers in attendance), who served at Grosse Isle, two caught the fever and died,—Richard Anderson, of New Ireland, and Charles J. Morris, of Portneuf. Three of the clergy took it in attendance on the Emigrant Sheds elsewhere and died,—William Chaderton, of St. Peter's, Quebec, Mark Willoughby, of Trinity Church, Montreal, and William Dawes, of St. John's. These five were among the most devout and efficient of the clergy, and their death was a serious loss to the Diocese. They left it however enriched for ever with the memory of their noble self-sacrifice in " laying down their lives for their brethren." Seven more of the clergy took the fever at Grosse Isle and recovered. They were Charles Forest, John Torrance, Richard Lonsdell, Edward Cullen Parkin, William King, Charles Peter Reid, and John Butler. The six, equally meritorious, who escaped unhurt, were, besides the Bishop, Dr. George Mackie, Official of the Diocese, Charles Rollit, Edward G. Sutton, Andrew T. Whitten, Narcisse Guerout, and Charles Morice. Let their names be held in everlasting remembrance.

Erection of the New Diocese of Montreal.

In April of the same year that saw the appointment of a Bishop for Red River, the S. P. G. resolved, " in compliance with the Bishop's urgent and frequently repeated recommendations," to take in hand the establishment of a See at Montreal. A special appeal was issued by the Colonial Bishoprics' Council, which was so successful that on St. James' Day in the next year, 1850, Dr. Francis Fulford was consecrated in Westminster Abbey the first Bishop of Montreal, and arrived in the Cathedral City on the 11th September in the same year. It was of a piece with the beautiful self-denial of Bishop Mountain's whole life that he gave up, at the age of sixty-one, as if it were a matter of course, the more wealthy, less laborious, and in every way more attractive portion of the Diocese to the new Bishop, a young and vigorous man, together with the office of Metropolitan, which he knew would be attached to it, choosing for himself the poorer, rougher and harder portion.

Bishop Mountain had completed his Fifth Circuit of Visitation about a month before Bishop Fulford's arrival, and he gives in his Journal of that circuit a brief statistical table of the progress made within the fourteen years of his tenure of the undivided See. The clergy in Lower Canada had increased from 34 to 86, and 83 new churches had been built,—31 of these clergy and 48 of the churches being in the new Diocese of Montreal. There had been confirmed 8,500, of whom about 5,000 were in that Diocese. The number of miles travelled, as roads were then, on each circuit of confirmation, was about 4,000.

THE SYNODICAL ORGANIZATION OF THE CHURCH.

The next great step in the progress of the Diocese was the organization of its Synod.

The revival of the Synodical organization of the church was, in many respects, the most important movement of the century. In this revival the Bishop and Diocese of Quebec took an influential part. After several years of correspondence, the Bishop brought about, in the autumn of 1851, a meeting of the B. N. A. Bishops at Quebec for a preliminary conference on this important matter. Of the seven Bishops then in B. N. America, five attended the Conference,—the Bishops of Montreal, Fredericton, Toronto and Newfoundland, with the Bishop of Quebec, as senior, presiding. The Bishops of Nova Scotia and Rupert's Land, who were unable to be present, subsequently gave in their adhesion to what was done. The Bishops remained ten days together closely engaged in consultation. The conclusions they arrived at were sent, in the first instance, to the Archbishop of Canterbury, as "a statement of their views in relation to the many discouragements and hindrances by which they were surrounded, which statement they desire to commend to His Grace's favourable consideration, as their Metropolitan, in the hope that he may assist them in obtaining relief."

The Statement is a most valuable and statesmanlike document, admirably calculated to be what it was, the foundation of all future synodical action in the Canadian Church. The subjects treated of, arranged under fourteen heads, were : the Organization of the Colonial Church, by means of Provincial and Diocesan Synods, under a Provincial Metropolitan ; Church Membership; the Canons, Articles and Formularies ; the Division of the Services; an Authorized Hymnal; the revival of the Offertory; the Exclusion of evil livers from the Holy Communion, and of those married within the Prohibited Degrees ; Inter-communion with other Reformed Episcopal Churches; the Religious Education of the laity and the Training of the clergy ; Provision for the maintenance of the clergy and the Restraint of Deacons from the charge of Parishes. *

As soon as the Archbishop's judgment upon the Statement was received, the whole was communicated to the clergy by the several Bishops. The Archbishop's reply was disappointing; he saw no hope of the legal impediments in the way of Synodical Action being removed, but he thought the Government would agree to appoint a Metropolitan. The Bishop of Quebec at once wrote to say that " a Metropolitan apart from the object of his presiding in the Councils of the Church

---

* The Statement is printed in full in Bishop Mountain's Memoir, pages 291–299.

would answer no good purpose, so that if Synods could not be had, it would be better for the Bishops in the Colonies to remain as they were, under His Grace's own Archiepiscopal jurisdiction."

The matter did not long rest there. At the end of 1852, the Bishop of Quebec was summoned to England, as the senior Prelate of British North America, to meet the Bishop of Sydney, the senior Bishop of Australia, with a view to removing the supposed legal impediments. Conferences of the Colonial Bishops then in England,—those of Sydney, Quebec, Newfoundland, Nova Scotia, Cape Town and Antigua,—were held, the Bishop of Quebec presiding; and afterwards joint Conferences of them and the English Bishops, eighteen of the latter taking part, with the Archbishop presiding. The result was, a Bill introduced by the Archbishop into Parliament, with Mr. Gladstone to take charge of it in the House of Commons, for the removal of the supposed disabilities. The Bill did not pass, happily for the Canadian Church, to the expansion of which such an Act might have proved a serious obstacle. An Act of the Canadian Parliament, however, was obtained in 1857, and the first Synod of Quebec met in 1859.

CONSTITUTION OF THE DIOCESAN SYNOD OF QUEBEC.

The framing of a constitution for the Synod was the occasion of an agitation extending over several years and attended with much bitterness and strife. An attempt was made to exclude two principles which the Bishop and the great body of the Church felt to be essential. These were, first, that no act of the Synod should be valid without the Bishop's assent; and, secondly, that the lay delegates should be chosen from among the Communicants of the Church. When the Synod met, its members were found to be practically unanimous in their support of the Bishop. These points once settled, there followed a time of unity, peace and concord in the Diocese, which, it is believed, nothing can now disturb.

In 1860, a Metropolitan See for Canada was created by Letters Patent of the Queen, Montreal being selected as the Metropolis, and, in 1861, the first Provincial Synod met in that city. The original arrangement agreed upon at the London Episcopal Conference of 1853 was that Quebec should be the Metropolitan See for B. N. America. Bishop Mountain however intervened and wrote privately to the Archbishop of Canterbury, declining the honour for himself and recommending the appointment of the Bishop of Montreal. In 1860, it was first proposed that the Bishop Senior by consecration should be the Metropolitan, but Bishop Mountain wrote so strongly against this arrangement as contrary to all ancient precedent, that it was dropped, and Montreal, by his advice, was chosen as the fixed Metropolitan See. The Synodical organization of the Church in Canada was now complete, and in every particular sound principles had been preserved.

THE ORGANIZATION OF THE DIOCESAN BOARD.

One more organization, and, in many respects, the most important of all in the healthy development of the Diocese, the Diocesan Board, Bishop Mountain lived to see completed and its work begun. During his oversight of twenty-seven years, the clergy had indeed increased from seventeen to fifty-three; but, of these, thirty-three were country missionaries, deriving almost their entire stipend from the S. P. G. For fully half a century this unhealthy state of things had gone on. At length, after long warning, the Venerable Society began in earnest to withdraw its aid, but upon a plan that threatened to be disastrous. When this was explained, the Society agreed, at the request of the Diocese, to cease paying individual missionaries, and to make its contribution to the Diocese a gradually diminishing block grant, which should be expended as the authorities on the spot might judge to be most for the advantage of Church extension. And it was finally arranged that a special organization should be created in Quebec, to which should be entrusted the management and distribution of the Society's annual grant. This was the origin of the Diocesan Board, which has been the instrument of doing for the Diocese of Quebec so splendid a work of financial organization and missionary extension.

The Board is composed of an equal number of clergy and laity, elected by the Church Society and the Synod; the Bishop is *ex-officio* President; and no act of the Board is valid without his approval. Two great principles form the constitutional foundation of the Board and lie at the root of all its success; first, an equitable Assessment of all the Missions of the Diocese for the support of the clergy ; and, second, the payment of this Assessment not directly to the clergyman but into a common fund, and the payment of all the Missionary Clergy out of this common fund.

The organization of the Diocesan Board was completed in the Synod of 1862; its first meeting was held on the 4th July of that year, its operations commenced on the 1st January, 1863. But the work it had to do, a work from which he always shrank, was reserved for younger hands ; five days later the beloved Bishop died.

This imperfect sketck of the ' great work of a great life, must now draw to a close.

SUMMARY OF BISHOP MOUNTAIN'S WORK.

The spiritual work that Bishop Mountain did, his devoting himself from the first with such absorption to the preaching of Christ crucified, and the conversion and edification of souls, stands out so prominently in his life, that it seems as if he could have paid attention to nothing else. On the other hand, so extended and complete was the organization of the Diocese effected by him, that it seems as if it must have engrossed all his time. He took charge of the Parish of Quebec, with its five thousand souls, in its infancy. Its gradual expansion into five distinct cures ; its Parish, day and Sunday-Schools ; its two Orphan Asylums, with their endowments and beautiful homes ; its Church Home for the aged and infirm poor ; its religious and bountiful care for the destitute and indigent, even to Rescue work among the fallen ;— all this was his work. Best of all was the sober, healthy, religious tone which pervaded the whole.

And what the Bishop did for his own Parish he sought to do and in a measure effected for the whole Diocese. The provision of clergy for all the English-speaking settlements within the Diocese, however remote or however small their numbers, even for the Magdalen Islands and Labrador, was the result of his own personal investigation of their needs. He never left any portion of the flock of Christ entrusted to him unquestioningly to others. " He fed them all faithfully with a true heart, and ruled them prudently with all his power." The result of this loving care was that he left his Diocese in the best possible condition with sound foundations laid on which others might safely build.

THE BISHOP'S PERSONAL CHARACTER.

There is little need to draw here a portrait of the character of Bishop George Mountain ; it stands out from every line of the foregoing sketch. " Applied to him," writes the present Bishop of Connecticut, " the line on Berkeley was hardly an exaggeration, for he did really seem to have ' every virtue under heaven.' " Every word of his own eulogium upon his father was emphatically true of himself. * There was a savour of piety and of genuine Christian kindness about everything that proceeded out of his mouth. His sweetness and gentle tenderness were wonderful. His thoughtfulness and considerateness for the feelings of others were only equalled by his forgetfulness of himself.

His charities were large and his contributions to religious objects systematic. Like his father, he made it a rule never to save anything out of his professional income, but to spend it all upon the Church. This trait was common to the first three Bishops.

Bishop George Mountain was what all the Bishops of Quebec have been, a true and loyal son of the Church of England without a particle of party character. In the maintenance of the distinctive doctrines and observances of the Church he was thoroughly uncompromising. He never gave way a single step to popular clamour, nor did he ever hesitate to come forward in defence of his clergy when unjustly assailed. He met with several very severe trials of his principles as a

---

* What follows is taken in part from a sketch of the Bishop's life, drawn up for the newspapers by the writer, at the request of the Bishop's family at the time of his death, and partly copied into the Bishop's Memoir.

churchman, but in every instance he calmly stood his ground, fought the battle and won it.

His death was what might have been expected after such a life, holy and peaceful, full of humility but strong in faith, thoughtful for others to the last, pouring himself out for them in intercessions and blessings. "The description of the Bishop's last days and hours," wrote his saintly brother Bishop Field, referring to a private letter, "was most touching and delightful. I have never heard of any person's departure respecting which I could more earnestly and sincerely say and pray, 'Let my last end be like his.'"

The blessed memory of his holy life will ever be the peculiar treasure of the Canadian Church.

He took cold, which rapidly developed into Pneumonia, on Christmas Day, 1862, from ministering to the prisoners in the Quebec jail. On the Feast of the Epiphany, 1863, he died.

CHAPTER IV.

THE FOURTH BISHOP OF QUEBEC :

JAMES WILLIAM WILLIAMS, A.D., 1863-1892.

The first three Bishops of Quebec were appointed by
the Crown upon the nomination of the Colonial Minister and with the advice of the Archbishop of Canterbury. The fourth Bishop was freely elected by the
suffrages of the clergy and faithful laity of his own
Diocese ; and was consecrated in his own Cathedral by
the Metropolitan of Canada.

This change in the mode of appointment was an or-
deal to which Bishop Mountain looked forward not
without anxiety, and had put on record, in his address
to the Synod of 1861, the following solemn and touching warning : " In our own case the principle of elec-
tive Bishops has been introduced, and the day cannot
be very remote when occasion will be given to put
this principle in exercise within the Diocese of Quebec. I hope the clergy and laity will be prepared,
when that day shall come, to act with a single eye to
the glory of God, to the salvation of souls, and to the
progress and consolidation of the church,—with an in-
violate spirit of charity and forbearance ; with an utter
repudiation of all worldly intrigue and partizanship,
all recourse to the arts of canvassing and caballing,—
everything in short which is described by the word
electioneering in the transaction of popular government
in the world." These affectionate counsels were not

forgotten or rather were probably not needed by those
upon whom this great responsibility was placed. They
had had instilled into them by the teaching and life of
Bishop Mountain himself too high a sense of the
dignity and sacredness of the Episcopal office to conduct the election by partizanship or intrigue. Never
was there an Episcopal election more purely, more
Christianly conducted. The Synod met on the 4th
March, 1863. Balloting began on the morning of the
5th, and continued till late in the evening, when the
Rev. James William Williams, of Pembroke College,
Oxford, then Rector of the Lennoxville Grammar
School, was chosen.

Thirty-one out of the forty clergy present, and thirty-
one out of the sixty-three lay delegates voted for the
Rev. Armine Mountain, son of the late Bishop. Eleven
of the clergy and thirty of the lay delegates cast their
ballots for Bishop Anderson, of Rupert's Land. When
it was found that neither of these could be elected, the
votes began to turn in favour of Mr. Williams; and on
the eleventh ballot he was chosen. Thereupon the
election was made unanimous.

EARLY YEARS OF BISHOP WILLIAMS.

James William Williams, son of the late David Wil-
liams, Rector of Baughurst, Hampshire, was born at
Overton, Hants, in 1825. His father's cousin, the
saintly Isaac Williams, and Archdeacon Sir George
Prevost, who had married Isaac Williams' sister, were
his god-parents. Thus the link of his connection with
Quebec was forged at his baptism, for Sir George Pre-
vost, whose father had been Governor General of
Canada, was an intimate friend of Bishop Mountain.
At the age of seventeen Mr. Williams went out for

4

three years with a party of engineers to New Zealand, where he met Bishop Selwyn, whose noble character and work made a deep impression upon him. Returning from New Zealand he entered at Pembroke College, Oxford, took a good degree, read for Holy Orders, and was ordained by the great Bishop Wilberforce, of Oxford, in 1852. After serving several Curacies, and two years' experience as assistant master in Leamington College, he came to Canada in 1857. The Lennoxville Grammar School, founded in 1845 simultaneously with the College, had, after a career of prosperity and usefulness, broken down and remained closed for three years. In 1857 it was decided to reopen it, and Mr. Williams was appointed Rector. The restoration of a school under these circumstances was, it need not be said, a difficult task ; but it soon became apparent that in Mr. Williams, Lennoxville had obtained no ordinary school-master. The school rapidly filled up. A large handsome new school was erected on the college grounds. And, in 1863, when the Rector was called to a higher office, the school was filled to overflowing with 150 boys. These were days to which all the Old Lennoxville Boys, who are fortunate enough to date within the period, look back with peculiar pride and affection ; and a permanent memorial of their love, and of the great services then rendered to the Lennoxville School by its head-master, was erected in 1888 in the Bishop Williams' Wing, replaced by the still handsomer Bishop Williams' Hall, in 1891.

THE TWENTY-NINE YEARS OF BISHOP WILLIAMS'S EPISCOPATE.

Dr. Williams was consecrated in his own Cathedral on the 21st June, 1863, and was called to his rest on the Wednesday in Easter week, 1892. During the intervening twenty-nine years, the Bishop won for himself in an eminent degree, by his able, wise and loving administration of his diocese, the confidence and affection of his own people, and by his statesmanlike ability, manliness, and admirable social qualities, the esteem and respect of all classes of the community.

He took up the reins of government, it will be remembered, at that point where an organization had been provided for carrying the Diocese safely, as it was hoped, from a condition of dependence to a condition of independence; from being largely a colony of foreigners in the midst of an unsympathizing native people, a colony supplied with the ministrations of religion, and the support of its ministers from the alms of the old world, to being a church deriving its resources, as well as its members from the people of the land themselves. It was an arduous task, and to the older churchmen of that day, a task full of anxiety and fear. "Our people are not ripe for the self-supporting system," writes Bishop Mountain; "we cannot,—I am sure I cannot—carry on the church upon that principle."

For such a crisis and such a work no man more admirably qualified than Bishop Williams could have been found. Always cheerful and hopeful, his wisdom and prudence never at fault, knowing when to venture and when to pause,—in short with all the qualities of a great statesman, he inspired confidence in everyone, and had, from the first, the entire body of thoughtful laymen in the Diocese, as well as the clergy, at his back. The splendid result is seen to-day of a Diocese emancipated. The Bishop's own last days of health were given to consulting how to do what his successor in the very first days of his Episcopate has been enabled to bring to a successful issue, namely, voluntarily to surrender to the great Society, on whose bounty the church in Quebec has from its first day depended, its last remaining subsidy.

GROWTH OF THE DIOCESE TO FINANCIAL INDEPENDENCE.

For full details of this truly remarkable expansion, the reader must be referred to the Jubilee Memoir of the Church Society, which left the printer's hands on the very day of the late Bishop's decease. The following is a brief synopsis : During the twenty-nine years under review, the Diocese has lost largely by emigration, and the city of Quebec, which may be said, if we except Sherbrooke, to be the only place of any wealth in the Diocese, has been, especially in Church population, very materially weakened in numbers and in wealth. At the beginning of this period, even in Quebec itself, there was not one self-supporting parish. Bishop Mountain had been Rector of Quebec to the last, and had spent the whole of his salary as Rector, some $3,000, in augmenting the incomes of the city clergy. Thus, by his death, the city parishes lost and had to make good to the clergy at once $3,000 a year. Outside the city of Quebec there were then thirty-four missions, the clergy of which did not receive on an average a hundred dollars a year from their own people, the bulk of their income being derived from the Society for the Propagation of the Gospel.

Under the wise guidance of the Bishop and the Diocesan Board, thirteen of the thirty-four missions have become self-supporting parishes ; the remainder pay on an average one half of the stipends of their clergy ; besides this, eleven new missions have been established. * All this time, the annual grant of the S. P. G. has been gradually reduced, until now a scheme has been proposed by the Diocesan Board and accepted by the Society by which the Diocese voluntarily relinquishes the whole S. P. G. grant at the close of the year 1899.

Perhaps the most satisfactory feature of this rapid growth is, that under it the salaries of the clergy, not promised but paid, have increased from a dead level of one hundred pounds sterling to a scale of from $600 to $850 per annum, graded according to term of service. Sixty new churches and twenty-nine new parsonages have been built. Local Endowments for thirty-five parishes, which now amount to $113,000, have been founded. A Pension Fund for aged and infirm clergy, begun twenty-five years ago, on the twenty-fifth Anniversary of the Church Society, at Bishop Williams' suggestion, as a thank-offering for the many blessings which had accrued to the Diocese through the Society, already has a capital of $50,000, under which pensions varying from $400 to $600 per annum, according to length of service, are now being paid. A fund has been established for helping the clergy to educate their children. The Widows' and Orphans' Fund now pays the widows of the clergy in the Diocese $400 a year, and their orphans, up to four, $50 a year each. The Endowment of Bishop's College has been about doubled, almost exclusively from contributions within the Diocese.

---

* The eleven new missions are Barnston, Brompton, Barford, East Angus, Fitch Bay, Magog, Peninsula, Randboro, St. John's Melbourne, Waterville. Scotstown with Lake Megantic costs as much as a Mission. Stanstead and Durham are also really new missions, inasmuch as they were both closed and destitute of stipend and taken up afresh under Bishop Williams.

Still more satisfactory is it that, side by side with this splendid provision for the material prosperity of the Diocese has grown the missionary spirit, nearly $4,000 is sent out of this poor Diocese to help in the missionary work of the church year by year.

COMPTON LADIES' COLLEGE.

Within this period also falls the founding, in 1873, of Compton Ladies' College.

To the regular routine of Episcopal duties, as carried out by his predecessors, several valuable features were added by Bishop Williams.

ANNUAL CONFIRMATIONS.

The triennial circuits for Confirmation were replaced by annual or more frequent visits, rendered feasible by improved facilities for travel, in the case of all parishes and missions, except Gaspé and the Magdalen Islands. To Labrador, he made six visits, going over the whole Coast with the Missionary in the open mission boat, from Cove to Cove, and, when necessary, from house to house, with never failing cheerfulness and patience.

VISITATION—CONFERENCES OF THE CLERGY.

In Quebec, it is the custom to hold the Diocesan Synods only every second year. For the alternate years, the Bishop instituted a system of Clerical Conferences, which were helpful in many ways, and embodied some of the best features of Retreats for the Clergy. They were held at Bishop's College in the first week of the Summer Vacation and usually lasted for three days, during which the clergy were the guests of the Bishop. The Bishop combined with them his Visitations ; the clergy were formally summoned to them, and on each occasion the Bishop delivered a Charge. Papers were read and freely discussed. There was a daily Celebration, and one session was reserved for subjects helpful to the devotional life. The whole was delightful and intellectually stimulating to a high degree. Latterly, owing to various causes, these Conferences were intermitted; but it was always the Bishop's intention to revive them.

ORGANIZATION OF THE CATHEDRAL CHAPTER.

The year 1888 was the Twenty-Fifth Anniversary of the Bishop's Consecration, and it was marked by the appointment of an ARCHDEACON, and the organization of the CATHEDRAL CHAPTER. The Bishop and his leading clergy had always felt averse to reviving the mere titles of such a Body unless practical duties should be attached to them. The difficulty was solved in a Canon drawn up by the Archdeacon, and passed by the Synod of that year, by which it was made a condition of the tenure of their office, that the Dean, Archdeacon and Canons should say the Daily Services of the Church in the Cathedral in regular rotation for ever.

The Bishop appointed the REV. DR. NORMAN, Rector of the parish, the first DEAN. The first CANONS, limited to four in number, were, for the city, the REV. A. A. VON IFFLAND, M.A., Rector of St. Michael's, and the REV. T. RICHARDSON, S.A.C., Rector of St. Paul's. The Canons Rural were the REV. J. FOSTER, M.A., Rector of Coaticooke, and the REV. G. THORNELOE, M.A., Rector of Sherbrooke. The REV. HENRY ROE, D.D., Professor of Divinity in Bishop's College, had been previously appointed Archdeacon, being the first who held the office in succession to Bishop George Mountain, who had retained it to his death.

Church Helpers' Association.

Another valuable Diocesan organization was instituted towards the close of the Bishop's life, in which he took a deep interest, helping it with his advice and presiding at the meeting at which it was inaugurated. This was called the Church Helpers' Association, the object being to do for the Diocese itself what the D. and F. Missionary Committee and the Women's Auxiliary were doing so well for the Church outside the Diocese.

Religious Unity of the Diocese.

Turning now to the progress of the Diocese under Bishop Williams in higher things, one feature at once suggests itself—its religious unity and freedom from party spirit. The two addresses presented to the Bishop at his Anniversary Celebration in 1888 made reference to this happy state of things, and traced it directly to the Bishop. The address from the laity of Quebec gives the following admirable expression to what was universally felt : " The brotherly union and harmony amid inevitable differences, so conspicuous in the Diocese of Quebec, testify to Your Lordship's administrative capacity, comprehensive sympathy and fatherly kindness ; while the spirit of diligence in church work which exists among us is the result, in a great measure, of this absence of party spirit, and of your own influential example."

Spiritual and Personal Religion.

The supreme importance of spiritual and personal religion was stamped, it may be hoped indelibly, upon the Diocese of Quebec, by its first three saintly

Pastors; and Bishop Williams always followed closely in the footsteps of his illustrious predecessors in urging upon his clergy to make the progress of their people in spiritual things ever first in their thoughts and efforts. Moving expression is given to this view in the Bishop's Sermon, or rather Charge, delivered to his clergy at the opening of the Synod of 1888, a Sermon which it could be wished were in the hands of every clergyman in the Dominion.

PAROCHIAL MISSIONS.

Towards promoting the revival of personal religion and deepening the spiritual life, much use has been made of Parochial Missions in the Diocese of Quebec of late years. The marvellous effects produced by Archdeacon Wilberforce's Mission, in the City of Quebec, in 1880, led to the appointment of the Rev. Isaac Thompson as Diocesan Missioner for the three years following. During the last year of his life the arrangements were completed with his sanction and under his advice and guidance for the second visit of a great Missioner from England, Canon Bullock, whose work in Quebec and Sherbrooke has been so remarkably successful. These efforts, after the higher and better development of the spiritual life, have always met with the most practical encouragement and warmest sympathy from Bishop Williams.

It is perhaps chiefly this character of the church, as evidently seeking first the conversion of souls to God and their growth in spiritual religion, which has made her work in winning those belonging to no religious body in the Eastern Townships so successful.

Bishop Williams's Preaching and Educational Labours.

There are many other lines of influence along which Bishop Williams' Episcopate has left its mark. His Sermons, especially those in the Cathedral of Quebec, where he preached regularly when in town every alternate Sunday morning, were always appreciated by that cultured congregation, and have been a real power for good. His labours in behalf of higher education, both as President of Bishop's College, and as Chairman for many years of the Protestant Committee of Public Instruction, have been incessant and invaluable.

His Personal Character and Influence.

By the laity, especially the educated laity, implicit confidence was felt in his justice, good sense and sound judgment; he was entirely trusted, and had but to ask for what he saw the church needed to get it. The spontaneity and enthusiasm with which a Fund, amounting to twenty-five thousand dollars, has been contributed to form a Memorial of him is a remarkable testimony to the love and esteem in which he was held.

His social influence, combining as he did so remarkably genial playfulness of manner, the kindliest humour, and an unfailing store of anecdote, with fine intellectual power and wide literary culture, was unbounded.

Eloquent expression was given, in the leading article of the principal daily newspaper of Quebec, on the day after the Bishop's death, to the public appreciation in that city of the many noble qualities of his mind and heart: *

---

* Morning Chronicle, 21st April, 1892.

" Bishop Williams was a lover of literature in its amplest sense. His mind was always filled with the beauties of the great masters of the ancient tongues, and, when among reading men, he never tired of talking of the sweetness and grandeur of the old odes, the pastorals, epics and songs that had charmed the days of his boyhood.

" He was a theologian of deep and far-reaching learning. He preached a sermon of eloquence, power and thought. His lectures were models of skilful composition. On public occasions he never uttered a misplaced phrase.

" Amiability of character was one of his virtues. Kindliness of heart was another. Generosity was a third. The list could be indefinitely prolonged. He was a man of unbounded charity for the shortcomings of others. He could not abide deceit in any form. But he had the heart of a woman in any case of real suffering or distress which came before him."

The Bishop's death came as a terribly sudden blow to his Diocese. The sense of loss was overwhelming. A severe cold, aggravated by taking several successive confirmations for which he was quite unfit, brought on Pneumonia. On Tuesday in Holy Week, he confirmed in the Cathedral; on Wednesday in Easter Week he died.

He was called away in the full possession of his great mental powers.

In his answer to the address of the Synod of 1888, he spoke of " the unwelcome conviction obtruding upon him that his faculties for sustained exertion were growing less." He added : " I shrink from the thought of hanging on with impaired powers a weight and a drag upon the Diocese ;" but concluded with the hope that " the failure of his strength to work and his

strength to live might come together." The Bishop's
wish was granted him. There had been no failure in
his strength to work, when his strength to live sudden-
ly gave way. The mental eye undimmed, the keen
intellect, the sound judgment, the beautiful play of
kindly feeling, the exquisite felicity of expression were
all there. His friends can think of him to the last as
at his best.

Christian people have a right to know how those appointed to teach them how to die, have themselves
met the last dread enemy. The beloved Bishop received the announcement that the time of his departure was come with the faith and humility of a true
Christian. His sufferings from the first were very
great and gave but little interval for the expression of
feeling; those intervals, and indeed his whole time,
was spent in prayer and meditation. His son, the
Rev. Lennox Williams, scarcely left his father's side
from the first, and on Tuesday, the 19th, administered
to him the Holy Communion. The dying Bishop gave
his solemn blessing to his dear ones again and again.
Especially pathetic was the scene when his little grand-
son, four years old, whom he tenderly loved, was
brought, about an hour before his death, to be blessed
by him. Amid all his agony, he insisted on raising
himself in his bed to bless the child. He sent a last
message to his clergy, exhorting them to be good and
faithful men. Again and again, with deep humility,
he expressed his sense of shortcoming in the discharge
of the great responsibilities entrusted to him ; but ever
added his firm and entire trust in the all-sufficiency of
his Saviour.

THE SUCCESSION OF THE FIFTH BISHOP.

With the close of the Episcopate of Bishop Williams,
the first Hundred years of the life of the Diocese of

Quebec were fast Drawing to a close also; but, before they ran out, the vacant See was filled.

On the 22nd June of the same year, the Rev. Andrew Hunter Dunn, M.A., of Corpus Christi College, Cambridge, Vicar of All Saints, South Acton, London, was unanimously elected successor to Bishop Williams, and on Sunday, the 18th September, was consecrated in the Cathedral Church, Montreal.

L'Envoi.

The story of the Diocese, its growth and expansion under the oversight of its first four Bishops, has now been told. It is a story, however imperfectly related, to stir the heart and nerve the arm, so full is it of noble deeds and good examples. For the churchmen of Quebec to have such a spiritual ancestry to look back upon is a priceless heritage. May those who come after, hand on this heritage to the generations following, unsullied and unimpaired!

APPENDIX.

—

The growth of the Episcopate in the Church of Canada, as a matter of exceeding great interest, is here appended.

Diocese of Quebec, including all Upper and Lower Canada, founded on the 7th July, 1793.

Divided by the erection of the See of Toronto, including all Upper Canada, in 1839.

Diocese of Quebec again divided by the erection of of the See of Montreal, 1850.

Diocese of Toronto divided by the erection of the following Sees, namely : Huron, 1857 ; Ontario, 1862 ; Algoma, 1873 ; Niagara, 1875.

www.ingramcontent.com/pod-product-compliance
Lightning Source LLC
Chambersburg PA
CBHW021228260626
47172CB00002B/654